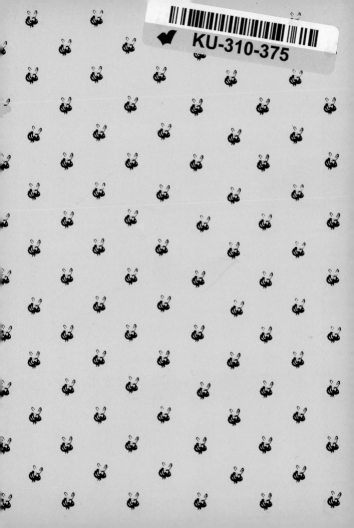

PIGLET
MEETS A
HEFFALUMP

PIGLET
MEETS A
HEFFALUMP

A. A. MILNE

illustrated by
ERNEST H. SHEPARD

PIGLET
MEETS A
HEFFALUMP

One day, when Christopher Robin and Winnie-the-Pooh and Piglet were all talking together, Christopher Robin finished the mouthful he was eating and said carelessly: 'I saw a Heffalump to-day, Piglet.'

'What was it doing?' asked Piglet.

'Just lumping along,' said Christopher Robin. 'I don't think it saw *me*.'

'I saw one once,' said Piglet. 'At least, I think I did,' he said. 'Only perhaps it wasn't.'

'So did I,' said Pooh, wondering what a Heffalump was like.

'You don't often see them,'
said Christopher Robin carelessly.

'Not now,' said Piglet.

'Not at this time of year,' said Pooh.

Then they all talked about something else,
until it was time for Pooh and Piglet to go
home together. At first as they stumped along
the path which edged the Hundred Acre Wood,

they didn't say much to each other; but when they came to the stream, and had helped each other across the stepping stones, and were able to walk side by side again over the heather, they

began to talk in a friendly way about this and that, and Piglet said, 'If you see what I mean, Pooh,' and Pooh said, 'It's just what I think myself, Piglet,' and Piglet said, 'But, on the other hand, Pooh, we must remember,' and Pooh said, 'Quite true, Piglet, although I had forgotten it for the moment.' And then, just as they came to the Six Pine Trees, Pooh looked round to see that nobody else was listening, and said in a very solemn voice:

'Piglet, I have decided something.'

'What have you decided, Pooh?'

'I have decided to catch a Heffalump.'

Pooh nodded his head several times as he said this, and waited for Piglet to say 'How?' or 'Pooh, you couldn't!' or something helpful of that sort, but Piglet said nothing. The fact was Piglet was wishing that *he* had thought about it first.

'I shall do it,' said Pooh, after waiting a little longer, 'by means of a trap. And it must be a Cunning Trap, so you will have to help me, Piglet.'

'Pooh,' said Piglet, feeling quite happy again now, 'I will.' And then he said, 'How shall we do it?' and Pooh said, 'That's just it. How?' And then they sat down together to think it out.

Pooh's first idea was that they should dig a Very Deep Pit, and then the Heffalump would come along and fall into the Pit, and—

'Why?' said Piglet.

'Why what?' said Pooh.

'Why would he fall in?'

Pooh rubbed his nose with his paw, and said that the Heffalump might be walking along, humming a little song, and looking up at the sky, wondering if it would rain, and so he wouldn't see the Very Deep Pit until he was half-way down, when it would be too late.

Piglet said that this was a very good Trap, but supposing it were raining already?

Pooh rubbed his nose again, and said that he hadn't thought of that. And then he brightened up, and said that, if it were raining already, the Heffalump would be looking at the sky wondering if it would *clear up*, and so he wouldn't see the Very Deep Pit until he was half-way down. . . . When it would be too late.

Piglet said that, now that this point had been explained, he though it was a Cunning Trap.

Pooh was very proud when he heard this, and he felt that the Heffalump was as good as caught already, but there was just one other thing which had to be thought about, and it was this. *Where should they dig the Very Deep Pit?*

Piglet said that the best place would be somewhere where a Heffalump was, just before he fell into it, only about a foot further on.

'But then he would see us digging it,' said Pooh.

'Not if he was looking at the sky.'

'He would Suspect,' said Pooh, 'if he happened to look down.' He thought for a long time and then added sadly, 'It isn't as easy as I thought. I suppose that's why Heffalumps hardly *ever* get caught.'

'That must be it,' said Piglet.

They sighed and got up; and when they had taken a few gorse prickles out of themselves they sat down again; and all the time Pooh was saying to himself, 'If only I could *think* of something!' For he felt sure that a Very Clever Brain could catch a Heffalump if only he knew the right way to go about it.

'Suppose,' he said to Piglet, '*you* wanted to catch *me*, how would you do it?'

'Well,' said Piglet, 'I should do it like this. I should make a Trap, and I should put a Jar of Honey in the Trap, and you would smell it, and you would go in after it, and—'

'And I would go in after it,' said Pooh excitedly, 'only very carefully so as not to hurt myself, and I would get to the Jar of Honey, and

I should lick round the edges first of all, pretend-
ing that there wasn't any more, you know, and
then I should walk away and think about it a
little, and then I should come back and start
licking in the middle of the jar, and then—'

'Yes, well never mind about that. There you
would be, and there I should catch you. Now
the first thing to think of is, What do Heffalumps like? I should think acorns, shouldn't
you? We'll get a lot of—I say, wake up, Pooh!'

Pooh, who had gone into a happy dream,
woke up with a start, and said that Honey was

a much more trappy thing than Haycorns. Piglet didn't think so; and they were just going to argue about it, when Piglet remembered that, if they put acorns in the Trap, *he* would have to find the acorns, but if they put honey, then Pooh would have to give up some of his own honey, so he said, 'All right, honey then,' just as Pooh remembered it too, and was going to say, 'All right, haycorns.'

'Honey,' said Piglet to himself in a thoughtful way, as if it were now settled. '*I'll* dig the pit, while *you* go and get the honey.'

'Very well,' said Pooh, and he stumped off.

As soon as he got home, he went to the larder; and he stood on a chair, and took down a very large jar of honey from the top shelf. It had H U N N Y written on it, but, just to make sure, he took off the paper cover and looked at it, and it *looked* just like honey. 'But you never can tell,' said Pooh. 'I remember my uncle saying once that he had seen cheese just this colour.' So he put his tongue in,

and took a large lick. 'Yes,' he said, 'it is.
No doubt about that. And honey, I should say,
right down to the bottom of the jar. Unless, of
course,' he said, 'somebody put cheese in at the
bottom just for a joke. Perhaps I had better go
a *little* further . . . just in case . . . in case
Heffalumps *don't* like cheese . . . same as me. . . .

Ah!' And he gave a deep sigh. 'I *was* right. It *is* honey, right the way down.'

Having made certain of this, he took the jar back to Piglet, and Piglet looked up from the bottom of his Very Deep Pit, and said, 'Got it?' and Pooh said, 'Yes, but it isn't quite a full jar,' and he threw it down to Piglet, and Piglet said, 'No, it isn't! Is that all you've got left?' and Pooh said, 'Yes.' Because it was. So Piglet put the jar at the bottom of the Pit, and climbed out, and they went off home together.

'Well, good night, Pooh,' said Piglet, when they had got to Pooh's house. 'And we meet at

six o'clock tomorrow morning by the Pine Trees, and see how many Heffalumps we've got in our Trap.'

'Six o'clock, Piglet. And have you got any string?'

'No. Why do you
want string?'

'To lead them
home with.'

'Oh! . . . I *think*
Heffalumps come
if you whistle.'

'Some do and
some don't. You never can tell with Heffalumps. Well, good night!'

'Good night!'

And off Piglet trotted to his house
T R E S P A S S E R S W, while Pooh made his
preparations for bed.

Some hours later, just as the night was
beginning to steal away, Pooh woke suddenly
with a sinking feeling. He had had that sinking
feeling before, and he knew what it meant.

He was hungry.

So he went to the larder,

and he stood on a chair and reached up to the top shelf, and found – nothing.

'That's funny,' he thought. 'I know I had a jar of honey there. A full jar, full of honey right up to the top, and it had H U N N Y written on it, so that I should know it was honey. That's very funny.' And then he began to wander up and down, wondering where it was and murmuring a murmur to himself. Like this:

> It's very, very funny,
> 'Cos I *know* I had some honey;
> 'Cos it had a label on,
>> Saying HUNNY.
>
> A goloptious full-up pot too,
> And I don't know where it's got to,
> No, I don't know where it's gone –
>> Well, it's funny.

He had murmured this to himself three times in a singing sort of way, when suddenly he remembered. He had put it into the Cunning Trap to catch the Heffalump.

'Bother!' said Pooh. 'It all comes of trying

to be kind to Heffalumps.' And he got back
into bed.

But he couldn't sleep. The more he tried to
sleep, the more he couldn't. He tried Counting
Sheep, which is sometimes a good way of
getting to sleep, and, as that was no good, he
tried counting Heffalumps. And that was worse.
Because every Heffalump that he counted
was making straight for a pot of Pooh's honey,

and eating it all. For some minutes he lay there miserably, but when the five hundred and eighty-seventh Heffalump was licking its jaws, and saying to itself, 'Very good honey this, I don't know when I've tasted better,' Pooh could bear it no longer. He jumped out of bed, he ran out of the house, and he ran straight to the Six Pine Trees.

The Sun was still in bed, but there was a lightness in the sky over the Hundred Acre Wood which seemed to show that it was waking up and would soon be kicking off the clothes. In the half-light the Pine Trees looked cold and lonely, and the Very Deep Pit seemed deeper than it was, and Pooh's jar of honey at the bottom was something mysterious, a shape and no more. But as he got nearer to it his nose told him that it was indeed honey, and his tongue came out and began to polish up his mouth, ready for it.

'Bother!' said Pooh, as he got his nose inside the jar. 'A Heffalump has been eating it!' And then he thought a little and said, 'Oh, no, *I* did. I forgot.'

Indeed, he had eaten most of it. But there was a little left at the very bottom of the jar, and he pushed

his head

right in,

and began to lick. . . .

By and by Piglet woke up. As soon as he woke he said to himself, 'Oh!' Then he said bravely, 'Yes,' and then, still more bravely,

'Quite so.' But he didn't feel very brave, for the word which was really jiggeting about in his brain was

'Heffalumps.'

What was a Heffalump like?
Was it Fierce?
Did it come when you whistled? And *how* did it come?
Was it Fond of Pigs at all?

If it was Fond of Pigs, did it make any
difference *what sort of Pig?*

Supposing it was Fierce with Pigs,
would it make any difference
if the Pig had a grandfather called

TRESPASSERS WILLIAM?

He didn't know the answer
to any of these questions . . .
and he was going to see his first Heffalump
in about an hour from now!

Of course Pooh would be with him,
and it was much more Friendly with two.
But suppose Heffalumps were Very Fierce
with Pigs *and* Bears?
Wouldn't it be better to pretend
that he had a headache,
and couldn't go up to the
Six Pine Trees this morning? But then
supposing that it was a very fine day, and there

was no Heffalump in the trap, here he would
be, in bed all the morning, simply wasting
his time for nothing. What should he do?

And then he had a Clever Idea. He would go up very quietly to the Six Pine Trees now, peep very cautiously into the Trap,
and see if there *was* a Heffalump there.
And if there was,
he would go back to bed,
and if there wasn't,
he wouldn't.

So off he went. At first he thought that there wouldn't be a Heffalump in the Trap, and then he thought that there would, and as he got nearer he was *sure* that there would, because he could hear it heffalumping about it like anything.

'Oh, dear, oh, dear, oh, dear!' said Piglet to himself. And he wanted to run away.
But somehow, having got so near,
he felt that he must just see what a
Heffalump was like.
So he crept to the side
of the Trap and looked in. . . .

And all the time Winnie-the-Pooh had been trying to get the honey-jar off his head. The more he shook it, the more tightly it stuck.

'*Bother!*' he said, inside the jar, and '*Oh, help!*' and, mostly, '*Ow!*' And he tried bumping it against things, but as he couldn't see what he was bumping it against, it didn't help him; and he tried to climb out of the Trap, but as he could see nothing but jar, and not much of that, he couldn't find his way. So at last he lifted up his head, jar and all, and made a loud, roaring noise of Sadness and Despair . . . and it was at that moment that Piglet looked down.

'Help, help!' cried Piglet, 'a Heffalump, a Horrible Heffalump!' and he scampered off as hard as he could, still crying out,

'Help,

help,

a Herrible Hoffalump! Hoff, Hoff, a Hellible

Horralump! Holl, Holl, a Hoffable Hellerump!'
And he didn't stop crying and scampering
until he got to Christopher Robin's house.

'Whatever's the matter, Piglet?'
said Christopher Robin,
who was just getting up.

'Heff,' said Piglet, breathing so hard
that he could hardly speak, 'a Heff – a Heff –
a Heffalump.'

'Where?'

'Up there,' said Piglet, waving his paw.

'What did it look like?'

'Like – like— It had the biggest head
you ever saw, Christopher Robin. A great
enormous thing, like – like nothing. A huge
big – well, like a – I don't know – like
an enormous big nothing. Like a jar.'

'Well,' said Christopher Robin, putting on
his shoes, 'I shall go and look at it.
Come on.'

Piglet wasn't afraid if he had Christopher
Robin with him, so off they went. . . .

'I can hear it, can't you?' said Piglet anxiously, as they got near.

'I can hear *something*,' said Christopher Robin.

It was Pooh bumping his head against a tree-root he had found.

'There!' said Piglet. 'Isn't it *awful*?' And he held on tight to Christopher Robin's hand.

Suddenly Christopher Robin began to laugh...

and he laughed . . .

and he laughed . . .

and he laughed.

And while he was still laughing –

Crash went the Heffalump's head against
the tree-root, Smash went the jar, and out
came Pooh's head again. . . .

Then Piglet saw what a Foolish Piglet
he had been, and he was so ashamed of himself
that he ran straight off home and went to bed
with a headache. But Christopher Robin
and Pooh went home to breakfast together.

'Oh, Bear!' said Christopher Robin. 'How I do love you!'

'So do I,' said Pooh.

Piglet Meets a Heffalump
is taken from *Winnie-the-Pooh*
originally published in
Great Britain 14 October 1926
by Methuen & Co. Ltd
Text by A.A.Milne and line drawings by Ernest H. Shepard
copyright under the Berne Convention

This book club edition first published by Grolier 1995
Published by arrangement with Egmont Children's Books Limited
Reprinted 1999

First published in this edition 1990
by Methuen Children's Books
an imprint of Egmont Children's Books Limited
239 Kensington High Street, London W8 6SA

Printed in Hong Kong

ISBN 0 416 16602 4